"Charmingly awkward, angsty and very funny. *Northern Soul* will strike a chord with all of us who have embarrassed ourselves for love" **JENNY PEARSON**

"A brilliantly funny and achingly real story that perfectly captures the life of a teenage boy in all of its awkward, cringy glory. I absolutely loved it!" **SIMON JAMES GREEN**

"A joyous read!" **LISA THOMPSON**

"Funny, sharp and full of the hilarious horrors of teenage life. No one can tell a story quite like Phil Earle" **KATYA BALEN**

"Snort-out-loud funny, heartfelt and mortifying in equal measure" **ROSS MONTGOMERY**

"Phil Earle's hilarious first-love story is for everyone who's ever dared to fall head over heels. Its note-perfect portrayal of discovering romance is guaranteed to make you laugh, cringe and cheer" **KEITH GRAY**

"[An] enlightening, original and oh-so-cringe tale of unrequited love" **LESLEY PARR**

"Awkward, tender and full of soul. A spin-the-bottle merry-go-round of a story" **STEVEN CAMDEN**

"A tale of young love, dating disasters and the ghost of Otis Redding eating kebabs, this was excruciating and hilarious – and I never want to be a teenager again" **ALASTAIR CHISHOLM**

NORTHERN SOUL

PHIL EARLE
NORTHERN SOUL

Barrington Stoke

Published by Barrington Stoke
An imprint of HarperCollins*Publishers*
Westerhill Road, Bishopbriggs, Glasgow, G64 2QT

www.barringtonstoke.co.uk

HarperCollins*Publishers*
Macken House, 39/40 Mayor Street Upper,
Dublin 1, DO1 C9W8, Ireland

First published in 2024

ISBN 978-1-80090-203-9

10 9 8 7 6 5 4 3 2

Printed and bound in India by Replika Press Pvt. Ltd.

This book contains FSC™ certified paper and other controlled
sources to ensure responsible forest management.

For more information visit: www.harpercollins.co.uk/green

For my dear old marra, James Gooder –
Now you one are we ...

Whilst some of the story that follows is made up, some of it, I'm afraid, is not.

Some of it happened to me ... I'll let you guess which bits. Be kind ...

CHAPTER 1

Before Carly Stonehouse, there were no girls.

Hang on, that's not true.

I do this kind of thing, you see. I make these big, daft statements without thinking. I mean, girls *existed*. Of course they did. I just didn't notice them.

For the first fourteen years of my life, I had other things on my mind. There was football. And mates. Well, there was Jimmy anyway, and he was the only mate I needed. Either he was in goal or I was.

We'd go to the cinema sometimes. And there was football, did I mention that? Life was simple. Happy.

Then Carly arrived and … well, bang. That was it. Game over.

I should have noticed Carly when she moved in on our street. I mean, the removal van was a giveaway, but what interest was that to me? A sofa and a microwave couldn't compare with slotting a penalty past Jimmy in the front yard. He was a goal up when the van drove past.

I didn't lay eyes on Carly till she walked into class a few days later. It was morning registration and, to be honest, I probably wasn't looking my best.

"This is Carly," Miss Atkinson said. "She's new to the area." Her words seemed to echo in my ears. For some reason, those boring eight words felt like a poem.

I swear the second Carly appeared I didn't just feel like a rug had been pulled from under my feet. The rug had been set on fire. With me still standing on it.

I started sweating. I stopped thinking about my fantasy-league football team. And there seemed to be music playing from hidden speakers somewhere in the classroom. But nobody else could hear it. Just me.

It wasn't gentle music. It wasn't someone picking softly on an acoustic guitar. It was a fanfare. A choir belting out the greatest love song ever written at the top of their lungs.

"You all right, Marv?" Jimmy asked from beside me.

I replied, but I don't know what I said. I think I might have dribbled. I can't be sure.

"You look like you've dislocated your jaw," Jimmy said, grinning as he dug me in the ribs.

I jabbed him back. Jimmy raised his arm as if he was holding an imaginary handbag in the air.

"Oooooh," he said sarcastically.

I was in trouble. I couldn't stop looking at Carly, but I couldn't have told you why. My heart felt odd. It wasn't hammering, but it wasn't beating like it normally did. I swear it wasn't just living in my chest any more. I felt it in my head, my legs, my fingers – they throbbed.

Was I already out of my depth only a minute after laying eyes on her?

What do you think?

I've no idea what the rest of the day's lessons were about. Our science teacher could have told us how to turn belly-button fluff into gold and my ears wouldn't have pricked up.

My mind and my eyes were elsewhere. I know that sounds weird, but I wasn't letching over Carly or staring without blinking. Well, maybe I was a bit, cos Jimmy noticed I was being odd.

"What is up with you?" Jimmy asked when we were halfway home.

"Nothing," I said. "What do you mean?"

"You haven't talked crap since school finished. Not even a fart has passed your lips. So what's up?"

"I told you, nothing," I repeated. "Just thinking about fantasy league. About the fact you're top and I'm not."

"Rubbish!" Jimmy replied. "I've been kicking your arse all season and you've still been talking crap."

I didn't know what to say, how to reply without lying. I mean, Jimmy and I didn't talk about girls. Why would we? But what if he'd worked them out already? What if Jimmy had a girlfriend and I didn't even know?

My head was starting to spin. I didn't know which way was up.

The only thing that saved me was that we reached the end of Jimmy's road.

"You coming back for a bit of *FIFA*?" he asked.

"Can't," I replied. "Homework." It was a crap answer as he knew we didn't have any.

"Oh, right," Jimmy said, frowning. "Speak later then."

"See ya," I replied, already lost in my head.

The walk home on my own should have done me good, given me a chance to clear my thoughts. But then I saw someone walking ahead on the other side of the road. The worst and best person it could have been – Carly.

I kept my distance, but my thoughts were so loud I was scared she'd be able to hear them. The other scary thing was that Carly seemed to be going my way. I turned right after her, then two more lefts and a final right, until we were standing on my street.

It was then that she spotted me, her face twisting into a look of confusion.

"You're in my form, aren't you?" Carly said. Her accent was northern too, but not from round here. Barnsley maybe. God, it sounded exotic.

"You aren't following me, are you?" she asked.

She didn't mean it in a serious way … I think. I swear there was a hint of a smile on her face, but it freaked me out anyway. My face flushed, my brain disconnected from my mouth and I seemed to lose all use of my limbs.

I said something. I don't know what. Her nose crinkled with confusion, and it was the greatest thing I'd ever seen in my life. I had to respond fast, with something witty – no, something hilarious or, at the very least, memorable. I heard my brain whir into action, searching the files for the right thing to say.

It took too long. Way too long.

Carly took a step backwards.

I panicked. I'm not going to lie. I panicked, and my brain stopped dead on the file that was open at that second. I felt my arm reach out and point. I swear blind I wasn't telling it to. Then my mouth opened. Again, I have no memory of telling it to do so.

"Home," I grunted as I pointed at our tatty terraced house. Not witty, hilarious or memorable. I couldn't have said anything duller. Or weirder. Until I spoke again.

Two words this time, instead of one. Twice the chance to impress her ... or twice the chance to confirm I was a total arse.

"Marv's home," I said.

What was I thinking? Why was I talking in the third person? Only losers with huge egos did that. I didn't have one of those, but after hearing myself say it, I was DEFINITELY a loser.

"Oh, really?" Carly smiled. It was a sad smile – the kind you'd give to a three-legged donkey rather than the future father of your fifteen beautiful children. "So we're ... neighbours," she went on.

And that was it. Carly turned and walked off.

I did not. My legs still weren't working, which was annoying, because it meant when she turned one last time, I was still staring at her. Like I was the man of her nightmares rather than her dreams.

I was out of my depth. I had to make Carly notice me. No, I'd done that already and then some. I had to make her *like* me. And that was going to be tricky. I reckoned I just might need a little bit of help.

CHAPTER 2

My first mistake was looking to Dad for help. Error.

The man wears Crocs for starters. And I don't mean he wears them to take the bins out or do the weeding. He wears them down the pub, with shorts and calf-length patterned socks. (Dad does wear a T-shirt as well – I was just trying to paint a picture of his bottom half.)

"They're the height of comfort," he says when challenged about the Crocs, without the tiniest note of shame.

He even has those awful badges on them. Two of them, on his right Croc: a pint of beer and a bag of chips. I thought about buying him a third – a simple turd emoji. But I couldn't bring myself to click "buy" on eBay. To do so would be to drag myself down to his low level.

Surprisingly, Dad is single. He's been single as long as I can remember. So long that I have often wondered if I was actually the result of a strange, sinister scientific experiment. The only thing more depressing than that thought is that scientists believed I'd be all right growing up in Dad's care.

It bothered me so much that I went hunting for my birth certificate a few years ago. Turns out he is my dad, and that he wasn't lying when he told me I had a mum, and that her name was Tammi.

It made me wonder if I'd have turned out differently if she'd stuck around instead of running off with a bloke from her office. Maybe I'd have understood how to talk to the opposite sex for starters. There wasn't much chance of that with only my dad as a role model.

I don't look like Dad. We have a different face shape and hair colour. I wear shoes on my feet that are badgeless and aren't made of some weird rubber. So why, why, WHY did I pause to listen to his music playing on the day that Carly exploded into my life?

Dad listens to music all the time. It's his thing. He owns a record shop on the wrong side of town, selling the wrong kind of music to other blokes that are the spit of him. You could open a bloody zoo with the number of Crocs in his shop on a Saturday.

I feel bad, slating Dad's shop, you know. When I was younger, I loved it. He'd sit me on the counter and play his tunes LOUD. But the songs were different then. They were faster, louder; they made me grin. Plus his customers would feed me sweets. Sometimes a customer would give me fifty pence just for being there. But over time, things ... changed.

Dad couldn't lift me onto the counter any more, and I didn't want to stand behind it every Saturday. His music changed too. Got weirder ... and sadder, like his footwear. It ranged from sinister, to unlistenable, stopping in the middle to collect a big old slice of oh-my-god-my-ears-are-bleeding-turn-it-off-please.

So when I walked into the house that day, after humiliating myself in front of Carly, Dad was NOT the person I was planning to go to for advice.

I mean, I was in love, and what I knew already was that there was only one thing worse than being in love and that was being in love with someone who you feared was out of your league. It felt as if Carly was Man City and I was Hull City. There was nothing I could do about that, and there was no one who could possibly understand how it felt.

I was stuffed. Or I was until hope came from Dad after all. Or from his music at least. It hit me the second I opened the door, like a right hook to the head that left me reeling.

CHAPTER 3

It was a man's voice. There was piano too – beautiful, beautiful piano – plus the occasional build of drums and double bass. But as beautiful as the playing was, it was all about the voice – a voice full of pain and longing. Whoever it was, he was singing about these arms of his that were longing for a woman he was in love with. Bloody hell – I both believed him AND knew how he felt.

I mean, I don't want to be daft or anything. I'd only met Carly six hours ago, and even then, "met" was a bit of an exaggeration. But I *needed* to get to know her, because if I didn't, then I was destined to feel the same longing this singer felt. I didn't know who he was, or where he was from. But as far as I was concerned, he was the only person in the world who understood how I felt.

"All right, Dad?" I said, taking him by surprise. This was already the longest conversation we'd had that week.

"All right, Marv," he replied. Alongside the surprise, Dad was definitely a bit irritated too, as I'd clearly interrupted his appreciation of whatever was playing on the turntable.

"Good day?" I asked. I couldn't just come out and ask who was singing, so I asked the question I had absolutely no interest in and kept my fingers crossed his answer would be brief.

"Not really," he said.

Two words. Couldn't ask for much better than that. But then he had to go and ruin it.

"Shop was quiet. No one's buying."

I wanted to say, "You mean no one's buying what you're selling." But then I remembered I needed something from him, so I kept quiet.

"It's as if no one has taste any more," Dad went on. "Like no one even knows what good music is."

I nodded as if I not only *understood* what he'd said but *agreed* with him.

"Like this, you mean?" I said, nodding at his turntable.

"Just like this!" Dad replied.

I wandered over to where he kept his wall of vinyl. Dad had spent half of his life putting it into alphabetical order. The other half had been spent telling me never, ever to touch it. There had been no danger of that, until now.

"So ... er ... who is this singing?" I asked.

"Who is it?" Dad looked shocked. Shocked that I didn't know the answer. "Who is it?"

"Er, yeah," I said.

"It's the Big O. The King of Soul."

"Elvis?"

Dad fixed me with a look that was so murderous I should have already been six feet under.

"No, you fool," Dad said. "Elvis was the King of Rock 'n' Roll. This is the King of Soul ..."

He waited, like that should've jogged my memory for the answer. All I could do was shrug.

"It's Otis Redding," Dad said, sighing and picking up the record sleeve. It had an old photo of a handsome, strong-looking man on the front. A moustache hugged his top lip, and he had a neat afro. He looked kind and wise, as if he had all the answers regarding what to do about Carly.

"Do you want to borrow it?" Dad said. "The record?"

This was a shocking moment. Never, in my fourteen years on Earth, had Dad even let me touch one of his records, never mind borrow one.

"Er, can't," I replied. "I don't have one of those."

"It's called a turntable," Dad said.

"I know. I don't have one."

Dad looked embarrassed, as if he should've known that. "I could get you one," he said cheerily. "Maybe we could even share a few records?"

He was trying – I had to give him that.

"No need," I replied. "You never heard of Spotify?"

The look on Dad's face told me that he had but that he wanted no part of such nonsense, so I turned and headed for my room.

By the time I got to the top of the stairs, I'd typed Otis Redding into my phone. By the time I opened my bedroom door, the King of Soul was already singing on my speaker.

CHAPTER 4

I'm not religious, but I swear I saw the light. Otis wasn't a king. He was a god.

It was like he was reading my mind, chorus after chorus, song after song. All of this came as a bit of a surprise, I have to admit. I mean, I'd not even noticed a girl before, let alone had feelings for one. I was confused, bemused, baffled.

I had no idea what all the emotions running around inside me even meant, let alone what to do with them, or how to make Carly understand them too. But here was a man singing from the depths of his soul who told me I wasn't on my own – that he'd had these feelings too.

And judging by the number of songs Otis had recorded, he'd felt it all the time. I couldn't help wondering if he was singing about the same girl every time or if Otis just fell in love a lot.

It didn't matter – he was singing what I was feeling, and he was doing it way better than I ever could. The only problem was, he hadn't written a song called "Get your act together, you loser!" I listened hard and I listened widely, not just to the top tracks on Spotify. I even went to the album tracks, the B-sides I could find, but there was nothing there that helped me.

I was exhausted by this point – an emotional, needy mess. It felt as if I'd found the answer, only to see it slip through my clumsy fingers. It may have been the emotions of the day, it may have been Otis's rich, buttery voice, but whatever it was, I reached the end of my tether.

"Tell me what to do, Otis, will you?" I yelled. "Tell me what to bloody well do!"

I sank back onto my bed, flicked off the light and fell into the deepest of sleeps. I should have eaten. It was the earliest I'd gone to bed in years. But rest was exactly what I needed. The only mistake I made was waking up again a few hours later.

CHAPTER 5

It started with a swear word. The muckiest, crudest word in the dictionary of swears.

It pierced the night and pulled me awake.

"DAD!" I yelled grumpily. I didn't know he knew words like that. Dad didn't even like rap, but it had to be him – who else could it be in my room at 3.37 a.m.?

"Well," the voice yelled back, "what do you expect when you leave your crap all over the floor? I could have broke me bloody neck, you daft sod."

It wasn't my dad. The voice was different, the accent. It was still from Yorkshire, but broader. Thicker. As if it had spent the night, and a lot of other nights, in a smoky pub.

I freaked out. I mean you would, wouldn't you? Waking up to find a stranger stumbling round your bedroom? I fumbled around in the dark for something to lob at him, but I could only find a bog roll. Dad always buys the cheap stuff, so it wasn't super-soft, but it still wasn't going to hurt whoever was trying to abduct me.

I flicked the light on, hoping to shock the owner of the voice, but it was me who ended up surprised.

In the corner of the room was one of the most handsome men I'd ever seen in my life. And he looked ... familiar. He was tall, six feet at least, with a neat moustache, groomed afro, and was wearing a black tuxedo and white shirt. He could have been going to the ball as Prince Charming if it wasn't for a long streak of tomato sauce down his front.

"All right, pal?" he said as he plonked himself at the end of my bed. It was then I saw the bag of chips soaked in ketchup in his hand, which explained the stain. At least something round here was making sense.

"Chip?" he offered.

I was pressed against my headboard with fear and shock. A salty, saucy chip wasn't the first thing I wanted.

"Er, can I have an explanation instead?" I asked.

He looked confused. "'Bout what?"

"Well, how about who you are and what you're doing here?" I said.

He laughed. "You daft devil. You know the answers to both them things."

"Er ... No. No, I don't."

"Course you do," he said. "It's me. You asked for help, so here I am."

I was confused. I barely knew who *I* was, never mind *him*.

"You're going to have to give me a clue," I said.

He was munching a chip when I asked, which seemed to annoy him.

"It's me." He pointed to himself, as if that would help.

"Er ..."

"Otis," he added.

It was the middle of the night and I'd been startled awake, so I wasn't at my cleverest best.

"Otis Redding," he said, properly annoyed now.

I laughed. I couldn't help it. It just didn't make sense. So I did what I always did when that was the case. I reached for my phone and typed *Otis Redding* into the browser. My hands shook so much that it took a dozen attempts to get it right. Strangely, the internet had no idea who *Ottuuus Rodwonnng* was.

But as soon as I got the spelling right, things got even odder. The photo that flashed up on my screen was of the man (minus the stain) sitting on the end of my bed, dripping ketchup on my duvet.

"But ..." I gasped.

"But what?" he replied, his mouth full.

To be honest, I didn't know what my next question should be. I worried that if I opened my mouth, two hundred questions would fall out in a jumble.

"Aren't you American?" I said.

"Does it matter?" he replied. He had a point. If he had been American, he definitely wasn't now. He was more Bradford than Boston.

Then a thought hit me, and I typed a question into my phone. The answer scared me.

"Hang on," I said. "You're … dead. Says here you died in a plane crash in 1967. That's" – I paused as I tried to do the maths – "ages ago."

"Well, that's one way of looking at it," he said, smacking his lips as he finished his last chip. "I prefer to see it differently. I'm a … what do you call it now? A sort of … genie."

"A genie?" I said.

"Sort of, aye. A love genie. I sort of hang around, listening out for folk who are sad, or a bit clueless, or, you know … daft … when it comes to love. Folk like you, basically."

There was no answer to that, to any of it, but it didn't matter – Otis was on his feet now, prowling around my room. "You got anything else to eat?" he asked.

"Why are you eating if you're dead?" I said.

"Fair question. It's not cos I'm hungry like. It's more … well … when I were alive, I were surrounded by women. Like a moth to a flame, they were. I loved them and they loved me. So put yourself in my position. Here I am, still around, but I can't talk to a woman, let alone get to know 'em, if you know what I mean? So food's all I have left. It fills the void."

Otis looked sad for a second, then added, "And I can eat a curry every night without putting on any weight. Winner."

He spotted half a piece of toast on a plate. It was at least three days old. It didn't stop him eating it.

"So," he said, "do you want my help or not?"

"What do you mean?" I asked.

"Look, I'm the King of Soul. I get a lot of people calling on me, asking me for help. For some reason, I chose you. But if you don't want my help, if you were just pulling my chain, then now's the time to tell me and I'll bugger off."

I didn't like the sound of that. But at the same time I had to know if he really was who he said he was, despite being dead.

"Sing something," I said.

"You what?" Otis replied.

"You heard me. If you are who you say you are, sing me something. Sing '(Sittin' On) The

Dock of the Bay'." I liked that song. His voice on it was amazing.

Otis turned up his nose. "I don't do requests."

"You're the King of Soul, but you don't sing?" I said.

"I didn't say that. I said I don't do requests. Anyway, it's my night off and I'm hungry."

I wasn't going to let him off the hook, so scanned my room and spotted a pizza box I hadn't bothered to clear away. There wasn't much in it. One slice of meat feast, minus all the good stuff that I'd picked off. I grabbed it, pulled off a hair that had landed on it and offered it to Otis as if it was steak and chips.

"Sing and you can have this," I said.

Otis sighed. He looked at the pizza, smelled the pizza, then made a grab for it. But I was too fast for him and whipped the slice away.

"No, no, no," I said. "Sing first. Pizza second."

Otis sighed again, fixed me with a stare that could curdle milk, then threw his head back and started to sing.

What a noise. I can't describe it to you, not properly. Not in any way that would do it justice. It seemed to get inside me, into my blood, and then it surged to every bit of my body. It made me think of Carly, which made me sad and happy at the same time. It made me want to cry, for god's sake, which was ridiculous, but I couldn't help it.

This man standing in front of me, he wasn't just the King of Soul, he was the Emperor. And best of all, he was northern. Somehow.

Otis kept singing for a minute or so. I didn't ever want it to stop, because while he was singing, I truly believed he was the answer to my prayers. He could help me make Carly notice me. Maybe even like me.

But he did stop, and I did feel sorry about it. I just wanted him to sing it again, then again and again and again, but I knew he wouldn't. Not for a slice of pizza that had a rogue pube on it instead of topping.

So I offered him his prize, which he folded into his mouth in one smooth movement. Otis barely chewed, just swallowed it, like a python does an antelope. Then he burped and exhaled the sour tang of mozzarella into my face.

"Right then," Otis said. "Tell us about this lass you want to impress."

"How do you know this is about a girl?" I asked.

Otis fixed me with a hard glare.

"She's called Carly," I said.

"Kelly, cute," he replied.

"No. Carly."

"That's what I said. What's she like?"

I had to think about that. Otis noticed.

"Are you wasting my time here?" he asked grumpily.

"What?"

"Well, you can't really be in love with someone if you can't even tell me what she's like."

"I can," I said. "And I am. It's just, well, she only arrived at school yesterday. She's new to the area. Her dad got a job here. She lives on this bloody street."

Otis smoothed his moustache with his index finger. "Good," he said. "Excellent. And there's your *in*."

"My what?" I said.

He looked at me like I was daft.

"Listen," Otis said, "it's late. It's late, and you're clearly overwhelmed with having someone like me in your bedroom, never mind your life."

He wasn't wrong there.

"So best get some sleep then, lad, and I'll have a think," Otis said. "Because you aren't going to impress this Keelly lass if you look as rough as a badger's arse."

"Carly," I said, before doing as I was told. But I couldn't work out if I wanted this to be a dream or not ...

CHAPTER 6

It wasn't a dream.

When I got up for school, Dad was slumped at the kitchen table, finishing his cereal. Otis was sitting beside him, watching jealously, almost drooling.

"All right, Dad?" I asked him, giving him the chance to say, "No, I'm not bloody all right – the ghost of Otis Redding is sitting right beside me!" But as he didn't, I guessed that I was the only one who could see our new guest.

Within minutes, Dad was off to sell miserable music to miserable people, and Otis kicked into life, emptying Coco Pops, Rice Krispies and Cheerios into a saucepan. We had no milk left, but that didn't stop him. Otis splashed in half a carton of orange juice instead, downed the lot and headed for the bread bin. Half a loaf and a jar of Marmite later, he seemed just about full and turned his attention to me.

"Right then," Otis said, "let's get back to this Caroline."

"It's Carly," I replied.

"Exactly."

I sighed but went on, "Last night you said her being new was good. That it was my 'in'."

"Damn straight it is," Otis said.

"Yeah, but how? What does that actually mean?"

"Your *in*. Your way in. God, you really are new to all this, aren't you? Look, all you do is walk up to her, look her in the eyes, tell her how happy you are that she lives on your street and ask her about her dad's job."

"Really?" I asked.

"No, you bloody idiot. Course you don't." He took this opportunity to whack me over the head with the Cheerios box. "I just wanted to check how gullible you really are. Start asking questions like that and she'll never look at you again, let alone owt else."

Otis started pacing the floor, pondering.

"I reckon her being the new girl plays to your strengths."

"Really?" I asked. That sounded encouraging.

"Aye, cos she won't know what a total plum you are yet. Any girl who's spent more than five minutes in your company will already be well aware of that. No, this is a good thing. An excellent thing."

"Thanks," I said, deciding not to tell him about my awkward encounter with Carly yesterday. I should have admitted it – I know that now. But he already thought I was a clown, so I didn't want to make it any worse.

My nerves didn't improve on the way to school. I tried not to speak to Otis as we walked along. People think I'm a big enough loser as it is, without seeing me talking to myself. Instead, I listened as Otis told me the plan. If you could call it that.

"The secret to impressing a girl is flattery," he said with total confidence. "Not every girl can be Zoe Kravitz, but if you can make them feel like they are, then it won't be long till they're falling at your feet, lining up around the block to go out with you."

I looked at him, unsure. The idea of girls lining up to go out with me felt unlikely.

"I've never been good with words," I said. "Not really. A football, maybe. But not words. Could I not just do keepy-ups in front of her?"

"Well, you can if you want her to laugh in your face. I mean, it's all well and good being a striker, but nothing beats a chat-up line."

I frowned. It sounded like the kind of advice my dad would've given before he gave up on life and love and decent footwear.

"Do you not trust me?" Otis said. "Cos if you don't, there's a greasy spoon over there with my name written all over it."

Surely he couldn't be hungry? He'd only just devoured that orange cereal soup and half a bakery. And besides, I needed him. He was Otis Redding for god's sake. "Yes, I trust you," I said.

"Right, good. So I'm going to give you three of the best lines ever written."

"Are they from your songs?" I asked. This sounded better.

"Not exactly," Otis replied. "OK, option one. You walk straight up to her, no pausing, no arsing around. You say, 'I hear your dad got a new job round here. I'm guessing he must be a baker ... because YOU are a cutie pie.'"

I stopped dead and stared at him. I was no expert, but I knew this was a terrible, *terrible* line. Carly wouldn't want to kiss me after this. She wouldn't be able to. She'd be on the ground either vomiting or laughing uncontrollably.

Luckily, my face must have behaved itself, as Otis went straight on to option number two.

"Girls like a clever lad. It's not all about looks and muscles, which is just as well ..." he said, stopping to give me a sad look. "So you could also try this. Get your book out of your bag and walk up to her as if you're reading it. Then, as you arrive, stop, look her flush in the eye and say, 'I do love reading, but if I could rearrange the alphabet, I'd put *U* and *I* together.' All you'll have to do then is choose the wedding rings."

I had no words. It was taking all the concentration I had to keep my jaw from hanging open in shock.

"Did you write that?" I asked.

"Bet your cute boots I did," Otis replied.

"The same brain that wrote all them beautiful, tender, classic songs came up with … that?"

"What can I say?" Otis replied, not hearing what I was *really* saying. "Wait till you hear option three."

"I can't wait," I said under my breath.

"It's the best one by a mile. Every word has been chosen to woo your love into falling instantly for you."

This sounded more like it, but I had my doubts. I couldn't help it.

Otis pulled himself tall and proud, his ketchup stain glistening in the morning sun.

"You stroll up all casual, but as you get nearer, you start to look confused. Start peering around her as if something's not right. Then, as you reach her, you ask the simplest of questions –

'Where's the thief?' She won't know what you mean of course, but that's OK, cos as soon as she says '*What thief?*' you reply, 'The thief that stole the stars from the sky and put them in your eyes, babe.' And that, my friend, will be that. Game over. Together forever, amen, and Uncle Otis's job will be done. All you'll owe me is lunch."

Now, I know what you're thinking. This was the moment. This was the moment for me to look this man, the King of Soul, straight in the eyes and say, "Do you know what, Otis, I don't think this is going to work. It may have worked in the 1960s. It might have worked when you had a voice like liquid silk ... but I don't think it's going to work for *me*."

But I didn't say that, did I? Maybe it was a symptom of being in love; maybe it was desperation. But in all honesty, it was probably more to do with being a bloody idiot. Because instead of running a mile, I nodded and recited that last option over and over in my head until we reached the school yard.

Carly stood there, setting my heart revving. She was with four or five other girls, already popular despite being the new girl.

"That her?" Otis asked.

"It is," I sighed.

"And you've remembered the line?"

I nodded. "But I'm not sure I can do it," I said. "I wasn't expecting an audience."

"What you on about?" Otis scowled. "It's exactly what you need! Cos they'll all melt as well as Carly. So, worst-case scenario, even if Carly says no, you can cop off with one of the others."

Otis looked properly pleased with himself.

"But I don't want any of the others," I said. "I'm not like that. It's Carly I want."

Otis shrugged. "Best not bugger it up then, lad," he said, before pushing me forward.

I stumbled up to the group of girls, a bit more clumsily than I would have liked. They parted as I tripped, ten eyes all on me. Several of them tutted. I'm pretty sure one of them said "Loser" in a quiet voice. I prayed to god it wasn't Carly.

I tried not to be sick. It wasn't easy, despite not eating anything before I'd left home.

"What are you waiting for?" said Otis in my ear, before pushing me forward again.

It must have looked as if I'd been drinking, which wasn't ideal. I needed to do something to set that straight, but all I could think of was Otis's last chat-up line.

Out of desperation, I walked up to Carly, fixed my mouth into a smile that probably looked more sinister than sexy and gave it everything I had.

"Who's the thief?" I said, too quickly.

Carly's expression started to change to utter confusion.

"Er ..." she said. "You calling me a thief?"

I panicked. "Who? Me? Calling you a ... No, no, course not."

Carly didn't look convinced. "Then why did you ask me who the thief was?" she said. "I'm not a thief."

I tried to laugh it off, as if she'd misheard me. "No," I giggled. "I said *where's* the thief. Not *who's* the thief."

"Oh, right," Carly said. She didn't look angry or pitiful, just confused, and made to turn away. This wasn't how Otis had said it would go.

"So," I said, my voice so high I sounded like I was six. "What's the answer?"

"To what?" Carly replied. God, I loved her. She was so ... patient.

"To my question – *where's* the thief?"

Carly looked at me. She seemed to be examining my entire face for some reason before replying, "What thief?"

She'd done it! She'd answered in the right way. I was back on track. I felt excited and astonished. So instead of taking a deep breath before going on, I launched into it. All ears were on me; Carly was looking me in the eye. I could do no wrong ...

"The thief that stole your eyes from the sky ..." I said.

I didn't realise what I'd said at first. The only thing that gave away the fact that I was a total plank was the laughter. And it wasn't a giggle. It was a tidal wave, an earthquake, a hurricane of laughter, all of it aimed at me with such energy that it literally blew my hair back.

"Oh my god," I said, furiously trying to think how I could fix this.

I tried to make a joke of it. "Ha ha ha, listen to me, will you? Stealing your eyes from the sky … What I meant to say, of course, was …" But then I stopped, cos I knew that if I tried, I'd make the same mistake all over again.

So I stood there. And blushed. My mind raced for something else to say. I hoped Otis might take charge and whisper something I could use. But he didn't. I was on my own.

"Well, it was nice … seeing you again … er …?" Carly said.

"Marv," I said. "My name's Marv."

And that was it. Conversation over. Carly and all the other girls laughed their way into the distance. It seemed to get louder no matter how far away they walked.

Otis moved in front of me and shook his head.

"That went well," he sighed.

"I suppose she knows my name at least," I replied.

"True. But I don't think she's off to get it tattooed on her wrist," Otis said.

I nodded sadly.

"Not to worry," said Otis, forcing himself to smile. "We'll just have to come up with Plan C."

I frowned and said, "Don't you mean Plan B?"

"Nah," Otis said. "Plan B is second breakfast. I'll never come up with anything decent on an empty stomach."

And off he walked, presumably to find the nearest cafe.

CHAPTER 7

I can't lie. The embarrassment hurt. In fact, it burned. I wanted to run away and lick my wounds until I was at least thirty-three, but unfortunately I was stuck at school. And at school, Carly seemed to be everywhere I looked – in every class, on every bench, in every lunch queue.

I didn't try to speak to her. I mean, what would I say? I couldn't trust myself to even say hi after the first and second disasters, so I just stood as far away as I could, blushing hard.

I didn't see Otis for the rest of the day, which left me mostly on my own. Jimmy was still a bit off with me about the previous day. I wanted to tell him the million and one thoughts I had in my head, but I just couldn't find a way to do it. Not without sounding daft.

So, instead, I kept my head down, licked my wounds and tried to have a normal day.

Afternoon school, then footie training. Surely that would give Otis time to hatch a new plan.

I returned home, sweaty, tired and nervous, and found Otis sitting in my bed, beneath the duvet, his hands cradling the greasiest kebab ever built.

"Make yourself at home," I told him.

"Well, I would," he replied, "if you thought about changing your sheets every now and then. Stink, they do."

I resisted the urge to tell him the only thing that stank was his food. It looked and smelled like no other meat I'd ever seen.

"I'll tell the maid," I lied, then asked what he was doing here.

"Got a fresh plan for you, lad," Otis replied. His grin was wide and surrounded by dollops of garlic mayo. "It's right in front of your eyes."

"You think a horse kebab is going to impress Carly?"

"No, you prat," Otis replied, pointing to himself. "Me. What am I?"

"After what happened earlier, I'd say a nightmare," I replied. "But I don't think that's what you mean."

Otis pretended to look hurt. "Hilarious," he said. "I'm a singer, aren't I? King of it, some said. If I ever wanted to impress a lass, I wrote 'em a song."

I was shocked. His idea wasn't bad.

"So you're going to write a song for me, for Carly?" I asked. "You could record it for her too. On my phone."

Otis was frowning, but I couldn't tell if that was at my idea or something weird he'd found in his pitta bread.

"Bit difficult, that," he said.

"Why?" I asked.

"Well, I've been dead nearly sixty years for starters. And besides, I can't be wasting my gold on just any lass who happens to take your fancy."

"She isn't just any lass," I replied. "You've seen her. She's ... lush."

"She's barely said a word to you," Otis laughed.

"Look," I said, "are you going to help me with the song or not?"

Otis thought about it for longer than I would've liked. "I'll help ... well, I'll read it. But I'm not going to write it for you. You want Carly to see who you really are, right? And like you for it – which, let's face it, will be a push. So it has to come from here." And he thumped at his heart, which only made him burp. It stank.

"I think I know what you mean," I said to him.

"Good," Otis replied. "I'll sleep downstairs on the sofa tonight. Let you crack on. And besides," he added, "stinks in here."

And with that, he tossed his god-awful kebab paper into the bin and left.

I sank down onto my bed and reached for my phone. I'd never written a song before, not even a poem. I had once finished a mucky limerick that a lad in our class started, but I don't remember it impressing anyone of the opposite sex.

It was going to be a long night and my room was smelling worse by the second. I didn't know what had been in Otis's kebab, but I was starting to wonder how long it had been dead before they cooked it.

CHAPTER 8

I wasn't much of a poet. Sitting up half the night swearing and stomping round my room proved that. But I was even worse with music. I'm not sure I could lift the lid of a piano, never mind play it. Luckily, I knew a man who could.

Jimmy.

Jimmy should have had it rough at school, should have been a walking bruise, as his dad taught there as well. Gooder senior was not a bad man, and he wasn't one of those teachers whose sole mission in life was to make your life a fresh hell, but he *was* a teacher. He was one of *them*, and Jimmy took grief for it, course he did.

Kids who'd had a bollocking from Jimmy's dad (probably with good reason) took their anger out on Jimmy daily, but he wore it well. He never seemed to get angry or frustrated, and I never saw him in a scrap. Jimmy was smart and funny in a dry way, but most importantly he was a musical genius. Drums, guitar, piano – he played them all. He could probably play them all at the same time, he was that good.

Jimmy was the man I needed. Once I'd apologised for being an idiot for the past two days.

"Is Jimmy really that good?" Otis asked me once he'd read the words of my song and had stopped laughing. (Didn't do much for my confidence, that.)

"He's the best," I said.

"Well, he'll need to be," Otis replied. "Because you know what they say? You can't polish a turd ... but you can sprinkle it with glitter."

I should have stopped then. Stopped and banished the idea (and Otis) from my life for ever, but I didn't. Because I couldn't stop thinking about Carly. And because this had never happened to me before, I thought I'd burst if I didn't tell her how I felt. I hoped, desperately, that the poem would do that. I had worked on it for so many hours that I'd lost any sense of whether it was actually any good. I needed fresh eyes on it, and they had to belong to Jimmy.

The thought of explaining myself to him scared me to death, but, as usual, it turned out I was just being a fool.

"Why didn't you just tell me you liked her?" Jimmy said. "I thought we were mates?"

"We are. It's just, well … I've no idea how to make Carly notice me. So I've written her a song."

"A song? You?"

"Er … yeah. And I thought you might be able to help me."

"I'm no poet," Jimmy said.

"With the music."

"What, you want me to write a tune to your lyrics?" he said, frowning.

"Yeah," I said, blushing. "I want Carly to notice me."

He looked at the piece of paper that I'd handed him.

"Sing this to her and she'll definitely notice you." Jimmy smiled. He smiled a lot, but I hoped he wasn't just being kind. "Carly does seem canny. And she's got herself a weekend job already, down the bakery apparently. Imagine that – a girlfriend with unlimited access to sausage rolls."

It was my turn to frown. Pastry was the last thing on my mind, but I did wonder how he knew so much about her already.

"Listen, Jim, everyone knows how good you are on guitar," I said. "And well, I'm not, clearly, so ... I need your help."

Jimmy looked torn.

"I'd say I'd do your homework for the next three months," I offered, "but ... well ... I'm in set three, and you're not."

"Don't worry about it," Jimmy said. "You're my mate."

"Yeah," I replied, "but there needs to be something in it for you too, so how's this? You write the music for the poem, and we busk it on Saturday, outside the bakery when Carly's at work. Whatever money we make, you keep."

"So, all you get is the girl?" Jimmy smiled.

"That's the plan," I replied.

I could tell Jimmy still wasn't convinced. The fact that he didn't answer straight away told me that. I tried to look calm about it, as if I didn't give a toss. But when he finally said OK, I found myself hugging him as if he'd scored the winner in the cup final.

"Mate," Jimmy said, "I'm doing this as a favour. But hug me again and the deal's off."

I let him go, despite my overwhelming desire to lick his face.

"I'll have it ready to rehearse on Friday," Jimmy said, frowning at my lyrics again. "All right?"

This was better than all right. It was magnificent. Otis had better stand aside – there was a new King of Soul in town.

Or that's what I thought then. Rehearsals proved otherwise. Singing was not as easy as I'd hoped. And practice didn't always make perfect.

CHAPTER 9

"Any advice?" I asked Otis as I waited for Jimmy opposite the bakery. It was Saturday morning. The moment of truth.

I wasn't looking at Otis. I couldn't stop sneaking looks at Carly as she bagged up cream horns and French sticks for her customers. She was a vision, even in a hairnet and apron.

"Sing it from the heart, lad," Otis told me. "I mean, the words aren't to my standard, but sing 'em like you mean 'em. That's all you can do."

This wasn't exactly advice to fill me with hope, but it was too late for anything else. Jimmy was coming, guitar and mini amp in hand. I'd thought he would just play an acoustic guitar, but in rehearsals he'd kept gently edging the volume up again and again. I hoped it wasn't to drown out my voice. Or my lyrics.

Otis backed away as Jimmy put his amp down.

"You ready then?" I asked, too fast. I couldn't help it. I was bricking it.

"Might help if I tune my guitar. And plug it in," Jimmy sighed.

"Oh yeah, course," I replied, and wondered if I should do any vocal warm-ups. I hummed a little. Jimmy side-eyed me. I decided against doing any more. Instead, I looked for Carly. There was no point doing this if she wasn't still around. But there she was, a glow surrounding her, though that could've been from the oven that kept the pasties warm.

I spotted her and smiled. She looked up, in our direction, and then she did the most brilliant thing. She smiled too. And that was before I even started to sing about her. This was going to work. It had to.

"Right," said Jimmy. "Shall we do this then? You ready?"

"I was born ready," I said. It felt like the sort of thing Otis would say, and I needed a bit of his confidence.

With that, Jimmy started picking at his strings, the sound rich and full. I turned to Otis, who closed his eyes and nodded along, liking what he was hearing. He wasn't the only one. People passing by slowed down or stopped to listen. They were smiling, loving it.

My nerves ramped up. I glanced over to the bakery and saw Carly was watching too, and she was listening, beaming. It was almost my moment. It was almost too good to be true …

"Play the intro again," I whispered to Jimmy, bottling it at the last second.

He didn't need to be asked twice. In fact, Jimmy played it even better this time. I swear, a woman at the front of the growing crowd started to weep openly at the emotion Jimmy's fingers were bringing out.

I watched gobsmacked as people started to walk up and drop coins into his guitar case. And not 10ps either – 50ps, pounds, two-pound coins! Then the crying woman stumbled up and dropped a tenner into it. It was at that point that I regretted telling Jimmy he could keep whatever we made. If he kept this up, I could have afforded plastic surgery to make myself totally irresistible.

But as I wondered what part of my face to have done first, I felt Jimmy nudge me with his elbow.

"You ready?" he whispered, and I nodded, though I wasn't. I was ready to run, but I couldn't, because people were watching. Carly was watching. So I closed my eyes and, with the deepest of breaths and a nervous fart I hoped nobody heard, started to croon the lyrics:

Looking through my window where
yesterday lay hope
It was only hours ago I thought that I
could cope.

I tried to keep Otis in my mind as I sang, and his advice to think of the emotion, what the words meant. Get that right and surely Carly would hear me *and* see me.

The years that lie before me are a
heavy shade of blue
Cos everything seems different
without you ...

This was it. The moment. The chorus where I let loose and told Carly everything I was feeling:

> *Without you, the stars don't shine*
> *so bright*
> *Without you, I lie awake at night.*
> *The dreams I had not long ago, now*
> *are dead and gone,*
> *I've drowned the light that once*
> *so brightly shone.*

I felt the words. Every single one of them. I felt their meaning. I felt the silences between the lines. I think I might have even raised my arm to do a couple of power grabs like them god-awful boy bands, I was feeling it that much. And if I was feeling it, then surely everyone else was too? Surely if I opened my eyes now, Carly would be standing in front of me, weeping openly, mouthing my name as I launched into the second verse. People would applaud as we embraced, cry as we kissed, and throw rose petals under our feet as I carried Carly away to start our lives together.

I felt braver and more excited than ever, and I allowed my eyes to open. I *could* see Carly, but she wasn't in front of me. She was serving someone in the bakery, but she kept glancing in our direction, a frown etched into her forehead.

I could see this so clearly because our adoring crowd had pretty much disappeared. The only people who remained were a couple of eight year olds howling with laughter, a straggly dog sitting with its mouth open, drooling, and the woman who had been so financially generous. She still looked tearful, which strangely made me feel a bit better. If I had affected one person, then maybe the song might have touched Carly as well?

The woman walked forward, wiping a tear from her eye. She stopped less than a metre from where I stood, sighed, then picked up her tenner ... sliding it into Jimmy's breast pocket.

"I'd dump him, love, if I were you," she said to him, and gave me a filthy look. "You could go a long way, but him ...?" And she shook her head before walking on, as if she was Simon Cowell's harsher big sister.

I felt my heart sag. I mean, this woman wasn't the target of my affections (clearly), but it didn't exactly bode well, did it?

"I'm sorry, Marv," said Jimmy. "I'll share the cash with you, honest."

I thanked him, then turned him down. I glanced over to where Otis stood, head in hands, and saw Carly leave the bakery and head in our direction.

I shook. With fear, with excitement, with the smallest hope that maybe, just maybe, my words had moved her, touched her, made her see the real me. Had she seen the person she wanted to spend her life with, or at least the next five minutes? At that moment, I would have settled for either.

"Hello," Carly said as she reached me. She smiled. Her voice, her teeth, the way she smelled of warm bread – all of it was perfect.

I went to speak back, to ask her if she liked the song, but she didn't stop. She just walked up to Jimmy and slid something into his pocket before smiling and walking on.

"Oh," I said, deflating faster than a football on a chainsaw.

Jimmy blushed. "Oh," he said. "That was just some change from a doughnut I bought earlier. Carly didn't have any 50ps."

"Right, yeah, of course. Well, thanks for your help, Jimmy."

I could see Otis walking off, his head shaking so hard it was in danger of falling off.

It was fair to say that Plan C had worked as well as Plan A.

Plan D needed to be a whole lot better. If I had the bravery to even listen to what it was.

CHAPTER 10

I was feeling sensitive about everything to do with myself: the way I looked, the way I sounded, the way I felt. Luckily, life was on hand to make sure I soon felt even worse.

I was told the braces for my teeth were ready to be fitted. In all the Carly excitement, I'd forgotten they were even on the way. But, oh yes, I needed braces, and not just the subtle, hidden ones. Oh no, these were to be rail tracks, top and bottom. My gob was set to look like a complicated Scalextric set. If a bolt of lightning hit my jaw, I could become the most powerful bad guy in the Marvel Universe. Just one who was single and lonely.

"They don't look too bad," Otis said when I got back from the dentist. He was sitting on my bed, a pile of fried chicken bones thrown on my duvet.

I tried to tell him he must be kidding, but I only managed to cover him in spit.

"Oh, bloody hell," Otis said, looking horrified. "This is really going to help with the Carly situation, isn't it?"

"There is no Carly situation," I replied. Or at least I think I did. I could barely understand myself in the braces.

Otis ignored me. Or he didn't know what I'd said. Either way, he carried on.

"Luckily for you, I heard there's a party happening next weekend. The sort of party where things can get fruity. In a good way."

I had no clue what fruity meant, but I had to admit it did make my ears prick up.

"Go on," I said.

"Andy White in your form is having it," Otis continued. "His parents are away, and I know for a fact that a certain lass is keen on going ..."

"Who? Carly?" I asked.

"No, Dua Lipa. *Of course* Carly. Which means you have to be there too."

How Otis knew who Dua Lipa was I had no idea. But there was one thing I *was* sure of.

"I'm not going," I said.

"You are," Otis replied.

"I'm not."

"You bloody well are."

"How do you know?" I said.

"Because you'll be giving her a lift to it!" Otis shouted.

"What?"

"That's right. You see, Carly's dad is away with the car. So she needs a lift there *and back*!"

I was panicking now. "But I can't drive," I said. "I don't even have a bike."

"I know that, numb-nuts. But your dad does."

"How does that help? My dad is a disaster. Have you seen him?"

Otis smiled sadly. "I have, pal. And it explains a lot, believe me. I've also seen him out there on the street. Talking to Carly's dad, laughing and joking."

This seemed very unlikely, but I let Otis go on.

"It's perfect. If Carly's dad is away, he might not even let her go. But if his new mate is in charge? Then it's go-go-go, and giving Carly a lift means twenty minutes in a car with her. To be yourself. No songs. No chat-up lines. You can just be ... Marv."

"And that's a good thing?" I asked.

"Well, it can't be worse than your singing, can it? And if you pass up this golden opportunity, could you live with yourself? Really?"

I thought about it. Yes, I was wounded. Badly. And I had a gob full of steel that made me look like a pylon. But I still liked her, didn't I?

Probably even more than before.

So before I knew it, I was agreeing to the plan. All I had to do now was persuade Carly that she wanted a lift with me. And my dad.

CHAPTER 11

Otis's plan was a simple one. At break and lunch, I was to stay as close to Carly as I could. (He did add that at no point was I to speak, sing or breathe until he told me to.)

I had to wait until the party and her lack of lift came up in conversation. Then WHAM! That was my cue.

"But be cool about it," he added.

I shuddered. At his use of the word "cool" mostly.

But I did as he told me. I "lingered", saying nothing, keeping even my breathing to a minimum until the party came up and I heard Carly say, "I don't think I'll be going. I don't have a lift."

At that moment, I felt a dig in my ribs. A hard dig. From Otis. I'm sure I felt one of my ribs crack, and I yelped. I couldn't help it.

Everyone, including Carly, turned to stare. I turned round too, as if it wasn't me that just howled like a wolf.

"I can take you," I said quickly, spitting a bit. I couldn't help it. I was still getting used to my braces.

"Sorry, what?" Carly said. To me. She spoke a full sentence. TO ME!

"To the party," I said. "A lift. If you like. You know, what with our dads being mates now."

She looked confused, but I went on.

"I'm sure it'll take a lot off your dad's mind while he's away, knowing you're safe and that." I shrugged, as if the idea had just come to me and wasn't a big deal in the slightest, despite the success of my whole life depending on her answer.

Carly thought about it. For longer than I wanted her to. Way longer. It was as if she was remembering the chat-up line and the singing and now the spit. But as nobody else had piped up and offered her a lift, she said, "I suppose so ... thanks ... So can you bring me home too?"

I felt Otis lean in close behind me. "Be COOL!" he hissed.

"Sure," I said. "After all, I know where you live."

As soon as the words left my mouth, I knew they were the wrong ones. They weren't the casual words of a lad just trying to help. They belonged to someone who'd been spying on Carly's house with a telescope and a notepad for the past three weeks. And I hadn't – of course I hadn't. I wanted to tell Carly that, explain myself. But Otis wouldn't let me. He was pushing me away before I did any more damage.

"I'll pick you up at 7.30 Saturday," I yelled behind me, still spitting like a wonky fountain. Carly just smiled weakly, the heavens lighting up as she did.

It was only when I got to the school gates that I relaxed and celebrated. I had a date!

"Don't push it, Marv," warned Otis, when I said this to him. "It's a lift. If it's a date you want at the end of it, we've a lot of work to do."

CHAPTER 12

It was party night. There were a lot of things that could go wrong. Dad for starters. He refused to wear proper shoes instead of his Crocs. But as he wouldn't be getting out of the car, I had to hope Carly wouldn't even see them.

"You won't say anything to her, will you?" I begged Dad for the seventeenth time as we walked to the car.

"My lips are sealed, Marv," he said as me and Otis got in the back. "I'm just relieved you aren't ..."

"What? Gay?" I said. "Dad, you can't say stuff like that!"

"No, not gay!" Dad said, totally offended. "Loads of the greatest male rock stars in history had relationships with men. I was just going to say I'm relieved you aren't as weird as I thought you were. For years, your music taste has been bloody awful, but lately … All that Otis Redding you've been playing." Dad stopped. I think he wiped away a tear. "Well, it makes me proud to be your dad …"

"Thanks. I think," I said, tackling the mountain of pizza boxes, McDonald's cartons and chocolate wrappers we'd left to pile up in the footwells. Carly would have needed thigh-high wellies to sit safely in the back as it was.

I bundled as much as I could into the boot, almost being sick when I found mouldy pizza slices and two chicken nuggets that seemed to have small plants growing out of them.

"Can we go, Dad?" I begged, once I'd finished. (He hadn't lifted a finger; nor had Otis, though he did eat some random fries I came across in the car's ashtray.)

We drove the fifty metres to Carly's house, my heart banging out of my chest, palms slippery with sweat. The panic seemed to have even affected my hair, leaving it sticking up in positions that defied logic and the hold of the strongest wax.

"Remember," Otis said in my ear as I rang the doorbell, "you don't have to fill every silence. With you, less is more."

"Thanks," I said sarcastically as Carly's door opened and an angel appeared. Well, if angels wore crop tops, leggings and Air Force 1s on their feet.

I opened my mouth to say hello. Surely I couldn't get that wrong? But nothing came out except a half-sucked Polo mint that I managed to breathe back in at the last minute.

"Tell her she looks lovely," Otis whispered.

"Lovely," I said. "You. Lovely."

"Not exactly what I meant," sighed Otis.

I smiled at Carly and gestured towards Dad's car. He was waving frantically from the front seat with a smile that bordered on that of a serial killer.

The next twenty minutes were awful, dreadful, the worst. We sat in the back, with Otis in the middle covering my mouth every time I went to speak.

Dad, on the other hand, had a plan. He knew I was mad about Carly; he wasn't daft. So he had prepared a playlist that he was convinced would impress her, one that would make her think I was the one for her.

The only problem was, my dad was single, with zero single friends, and last had a date shortly after the final dinosaur froze its nuts off. His music was not our music, and it definitely didn't help when he started singing along. I swear at one point he was trying to do harmonies.

When we arrived at Andy's house, I literally threw myself out of the car. Carly thanked my dad for the lift, classy as ever.

"No problem," Dad said with a beam, thinking he'd done well. "I'll see you in a few hours. Don't do anything I wouldn't do." And he winked at us both. BOTH. It was at this moment I realised he really *was* my dad. And I wasn't sure who I hated most. Me – or him.

I didn't want to make small talk with Carly as we went in, but if I said nothing I'd seem as weird as Dad.

"I'm glad we were able to bring you," I said, smiling without showing my teeth, just in case I had a bit of food stuck in my braces.

"Me too," Carly replied. "Your dad seems … nice."

God, she had that wrong.

"But," Carly added, "you do need to sort out his shoes. Crocs are for little kids on the beach. Not full-grown adults."

"Yes!" I replied, way too loudly. "I totally agree. We've got SO much in common."

Carly made a noise. I wasn't sure if she was agreeing with me or being sick in her mouth. All I knew was that she walked ahead.

"See you in a bit," Carly yelled, looking happy to be free.

I waved, crushed. Unsurprisingly, twenty minutes in the car with my dad and his hideous shoe choice had not done me any favours.

CHAPTER 13

Two hours in and the party had well and truly started ... for everyone else, at least.

It wasn't meant to be a massive thing, but word had got out, as it always did. And now there were teenagers crammed into every room in the house.

There were smashed ornaments, footprints halfway up the wall and more than a suspicion of booze hidden about the place.

I was considering getting my dad to collect me, but then remembered I had to take Carly home too, though I hadn't seen her in an hour.

I was wandering glumly from room to room when Otis grabbed my arm and pulled me into the lounge.

"Spin the bottle!" he yelled in my ear. There were new stains down his shirt.

"What?" I whispered. I didn't want people thinking I was talking to myself.

"Spin the bottle," Otis repeated. "Starting now. Sit in the circle and leave the rest to me."

I wanted to run. Sprint. Disappear. There were a dozen kids from my year, including Jimmy and Carly, sitting in a circle with an empty wine bottle laid in the middle.

I knew what this meant. Everyone would spin the bottle in turn and have to get off with whoever it landed on.

There was no way my spin would land on Carly. Not a chance. It'd probably stop between two people and I'd have to kiss myself in the mirror instead.

Otis thought otherwise and pushed me to my knees.

It was awful. One by one, everyone had a turn. Everyone got excited. Or disgusted. But everyone went with it. The only good thing was that Carly hadn't had a turn or been landed on yet.

Finally, the bottle was mine. I gulped. I'd never kissed anyone in my life. Just the back of my hand, and that definitely didn't count. More importantly, I didn't want to kiss anyone unless it was Carly.

"Go on, Marv," Jimmy said. Others joined in.

I had no choice. So I spun the bottle hard. So hard that I reckoned by the time it stopped, there'd be a chance we'd all have died of old age.

I watched the bottle blur in front of my eyes. This was murder. It slowed. It was nowhere near Carly. I wanted to weep. It was going to stop on the other side of the circle from her. No!

But then, from nowhere, my guardian angel took control. My guardian angel who just happened to be the greatest soul singer ever, dressed in a stained suit.

Otis jumped into the circle, bent his knees and delicately kept the bottle moving.

"Whoa!" Jimmy cried. "It's speeding up!"

There were cries of shock as this weird, magical thing happened before our eyes. Only I could see Otis, who was concentrating hard as he made sure the bottle stopped smack bang in front of Carly.

Which it did. Sweet Lord. I wanted to both celebrate and sprint in the opposite direction at exactly the same time.

"How much do you love me?" Otis asked.

I couldn't answer him. Not without everyone thinking I was a weirdo, talking to fresh air. So instead, I climbed to my feet and walked towards Carly nervously.

Everyone whooped. Only Jimmy didn't look too happy about it.

I reached her. "Are you OK with this?" I asked. It felt rude to just, well, get cracking.

"Those are the rules," Carly said, and shrugged. Her words did little to suggest she was feeling any kind of burning desire for me.

I took her hands. Was that what you did? I hadn't a clue. I did it anyway. Then I closed my eyes and leaned in, until ... well, we were kissing.

And it was ... amazing. I'll spare you the details, but believe me, it was epic. And I aced it. How do I know? Cos it didn't stop. Everyone else's ended after ten or fifteen seconds, but ours went on for thirty seconds, a minute, maybe longer.

It had nothing to do with Otis. He was running around the room, whooping like a kid who'd eaten sixteen bags of Haribo. Carly ... seemed ... to ... be ... enjoying it.

I tried not to think about it. If I did, I'd balls the kiss up. I knew I would. So I changed nothing, just did what I was already doing.

My mind started racing. Was this it? My way in? Would she think of me differently? Would Carly want to see me again? Her hands snaked round my back, suggesting so. It was hard to think straight, and Otis wasn't helping. He was shouting so loud now and running so fast that I thought he'd hurt himself.

And he did.

Otis ran flat out into my back, sending both me and Carly tumbling to the floor, still kissing, with me spreadeagled on top of her.

"Steady on, Marv lad!" one of the others yelled. Some people laughed, but not me, as the kiss didn't stop. The only difference was that Carly didn't seem to be enjoying it now. In fact, she let out a muffled scream. The only thing was, she was still kissing me as she did it.

It was confusing. As mixed a message as she could give. Even so, I tried to stop. But that's when I realised *why* Carly was screaming. Her mouth was stuck to mine. Not in a "true-love" way, but in an "oh-my-god-her-top-lip-has-caught-in-my-braces" kind of way. I panicked. Wouldn't you?

Otis hadn't prepared me for this. He hadn't prepared me for any of it. He'd just thrown me off the highest diving board there was and expected me to swim. I tried to pull away, gently, but Carly screamed louder and said something no one could understand.

Fortunately (or maybe unfortunately), Jimmy saw what had happened and said it out loud.

"Oh my god, her lip's caught on Marv's braces!"

The awful thing was at first no one helped Carly. Instead, everyone pulled their phones out and started filming it. That's when I *did* panic and pulled away again, faster this time, which made Carly scream and whack my shoulder.

"STAY STILL!" she yelped, or I think that was what she said.

Luckily for Carly, Jimmy took control of the situation, much like his teacher dad would have done. He carefully, almost tenderly, removed her lip from my brace. Carly fell back in a heap, and Jimmy caught her (of course he did). I was fine, not bleeding, just embarrassed and ashamed. But poor Carly wasn't so lucky. There was blood, and yelling, and accusations from those watching.

"What did you do, Marv?" yelled one voice.

"VAMPIRE!" yelled another, which didn't calm the situation.

"I'M SORRY," I yelled as I leaned forward to Carly. "It wasn't me. It was my braces."

With hindsight, this wasn't a great thing to say. It made it sound as if my braces had a mind of their own, as if they were something out of a horror film and had come alive to eat the rest of the human race.

I didn't know what to do. I looked for Otis, who was tiptoeing out of the room, hoping I wouldn't notice. I wanted to follow him, to tell him his clumsiness had cost me the most beautiful woman on the planet. But chasing someone that no one else could see and giving them a kicking didn't seem a good idea, especially when the girl I'd made bleed was weeping in front of me.

"Can I get you a plaster or a tissue or something?" I asked her. She didn't look *as* cross now – just livid instead of murderous.

Jimmy answered for her. "I'd give Carly some space if I were you, Marv. I mean, it must have been a bit of a shock."

I looked around. A few people nodded, others shot me daggers, while all the rest were uploading their footage to TikTok.

This was my time to retreat. So I did. I found an empty bedroom with a big wardrobe and I hid inside. I'd stay there until my last breath or until my dad arrived. I hadn't decided which yet. I was too ashamed.

CHAPTER 14

The good news was Carly found love that night. Or lust at least.

I would have settled for either with her, but sadly Carly's feelings weren't aimed in my direction.

They were aimed at Jimmy. I knew this because Dad ended up giving, me, Carly *and* Jimmy a lift home.

THE HUMILIATION.

They tumbled into the back seat, kissing. Either that or Jimmy was a doctor who'd managed to stem Carly's bleeding by sucking endlessly on her top lip.

"Oh," said Dad, flashing me a confused look. "Oh, right. Hello, Jimmy pal."

Jimmy waved without ending the kiss. I tried to get into the passenger seat, away from the mating couple, only to see Otis already sitting there.

"Don't you dare sit on me," Otis snarled. I didn't know why *he* was so cross. He was to blame for all this. If he hadn't knocked me over, it would've been *me* in Jimmy's place.

I lifted my eyes to the heavens. I couldn't shout at Otis, as much as I wanted to. Dad would have thought I was talking to him, and I didn't fancy walking the ten miles home.

Instead, I got in the back seat like a weirdo, next to Jimmy and Carly. At least it stopped them doing their "thing".

"Er ... can't you sit in the front, mate?" Jimmy asked. He wasn't being rude. He must have thought I was the world's biggest perv.

"I would." I smiled weakly. "But the seatbelt doesn't work."

"Yes it does," said Dad, way too fast.

"No it doesn't!" I yelled. "So put some music on and drive, will you?"

I'm not sure why, but Dad did as he was told. Maybe it was the pleading panic in my eyes. In fact, Dad drove fast and wild, braking too quickly at times and swerving round corners. This stopped the other two snogging so viciously, but it wasn't ideal when Jimmy ended up sitting on *my* lap at one point.

Finally, eventually, the humiliation was over, and we pulled up outside Carly's house. All the lights were off.

"Shall I take you home, Jimmy lad?" Dad asked.

"Oh, there's no need," Carly interrupted. "My mum can take him … she'll be home in an hour or two."

And that was it – the final bullet to my already tattered heart. Jimmy got to go into an empty house with the girl of my dreams, who was clearly nuts about him.

I let out a moan. I didn't mean to – I couldn't help it.

"Pull yourself together, Marv, will you?" Otis sighed from the front.

"Leave me alone, will you?" I yelped at him. I didn't mean to say it, but I was at my wits' end. EVERYTHING had gone wrong.

Jimmy and Carly looked shocked. Then confused. They got out. Quickly.

"Thanks for the lift, sir," Carly said, smiling at my dad. "Look after Marv, eh?"

Dad nodded and pulled away.

"Well," said Otis, "at least she remembers your name now."

CHAPTER 15

Otis was no longer the king.

He wasn't the prince, duke, earl or viscount.

Otis was nothing to me. Nothing. I wished I'd never heard of him. I wished I'd never asked for his help.

I told him as much.

"Bit ungrateful," Otis sighed as he searched my room for something to eat.

"No, it's not!" I yelled back, not caring if my dad heard through the walls. He already thought I'd lost my mind. "You've wrecked it. Ruined it. All of it."

"All of what?"

"Carly, my reputation, my friendships," I said. "All of it!"

"If it wasn't for me, the bottle would have spun onto someone you didn't fancy," Otis said.

"If it wasn't for YOU," I replied, "I'd still be kissing Carly in her otherwise empty house! But because of you, I nearly ripped her top lip off!"

"It was just a surface wound," Otis said. "Didn't stop Carly getting to know Jimmy, did it? I thought he was your best mate?"

I looked for something to throw but realised it would just pass straight through Otis. He didn't exist. He wasn't real. He was a figment of my imagination. Or a genie, or something.

"I wish I'd asked Ed bloody Sheeran for help," I shouted, which showed how truly desperate I was.

"Then why didn't you?" Otis yelled back. "Because he's a ginger? Bit offensive, that."

"I didn't ask him because his songs are corny as, and yours aren't," I said. "I asked you because I thought you understood me. I thought your lyrics spoke for me!"

Otis looked happy at this, which didn't help. Here I was, yelling in my own house. Meanwhile the girl of my dreams was down the road with my best pal, and the only company I had was a long-dead singer and a dad with no fashion sense whatsoever.

"I'd like you to leave now," I said to Otis as calmly as I could.

Otis looked gutted. "Do you mean that?" he said. His top lip wobbled.

"I do."

"Cos once I'm gone, I can't come back." Otis was laying it on thick.

"Good," I said. "I'll do better on my own. Without you."

"What, like the title of that song you wrote?" He looked as if he was going to laugh.

"GET OUT!" I screamed. I swear the walls shook.

"All right, all right, I know when I'm not wanted," Otis said.

He opened the door, then stopped. "Lend me a fiver for a cab?" he asked.

I shook my head.

"How about a tenner for a pizza then?" he begged, dead serious.

"I said, leave!"

And he did. Otis gave me a sad smile and a wink, then started whistling, like that bit in "(Sittin' On) The Dock of the Bay".

"I'll see you, Marv lad," he said.

"No you won't," I replied, and lay on my bed.

When I looked up next, Otis had left the building.

CHAPTER 16

Life went back to normal.

Actually, that's a lie. It's impossible to go back to normal when the worst moment of your life becomes a GIF, a reel, a meme.

That footage of me and Carly as co-joined lovers went viral on every platform imaginable.

I was famous. Only it was the worst kind of fame.

It didn't seem to bother Carly. She and Jimmy went on ... and on ... and on. She's met his parents, her his. As far as I know he's already proposed to her in secret and they're going to have seven kids and a Labrador called ... I don't know. I always give up when I get to that bit before the humiliation gets too great, but I know they're properly into each other. Jimmy and I are still mates too. I mean, none of this was his fault. I suppose I almost pushed them together.

The attention didn't seem to bother Carly. It slid off her but stuck to me. I was the lad with the problem. I was the one who got tagged in every time the memes did the rounds. I even got an email asking me to go on daytime telly. I don't know how they tracked me down, but strangely enough I didn't reply.

I lived a simple life. I cut my hair, tried to grow a moustache (that was a mistake) and went back to my life before Carly. Back to footie and *Match of the Day*. I didn't listen to any music, especially not Otis's. Every song reminded me of Carly.

I didn't stop thinking about her though. To do that would mean I never felt anything in the first place, and I did. She was still all kinds of ace; I just knew I had no chance. With every month that passed, the feelings I had for her seemed to have the edges shaved off them. Carly was a pebble to my heart instead of a jagged rock.

I only knew I was ready to move on about six or seven months later. I was on my way home on the bus, alone as usual. It was packed. The only empty seat on the top deck was next to me, and plenty of girls chose to go back downstairs to stand instead of sitting there. They didn't want to be bitten, after all.

About fifteen minutes from home, something happened. Just like that. Wham. No warning. Nothing. I needed a siren – some sort of alarm to tell me not to be my usual clumsy, stupid self. But it didn't work like that. Course it didn't.

"Can I sit next to you?" a voice asked.

I looked up.

It was a girl. My age. Never seen her before in my life. Different school uniform.

She saw my face for the first time but … didn't move away.

The girl sat down instead. And sighed. She looked sad. Tired. Weary. I knew how that felt.

I reached for my AirPods in my pocket for the first time in ages. Not cos I wanted to listen to music, but cos I didn't want to say anything daft to her. I didn't want to chat her up. I'd learned that lesson.

But the AirPods were dead of course. No battery. It was my time to sigh.

"You look like I feel," the girl said out of nowhere.

I checked that she was actually talking to me. She was. I panicked. But I said nothing, my lips tight.

"Tough day?" she asked.

I wanted to reply but didn't want to say the wrong thing.

We sat in silence. It felt ridiculous, like I was being rude. I had to say something.

"Tough life," I replied.

She nodded wisely. "You and me both."

Then she did the weirdest and most brilliant thing. She reached into her pocket and brought out her own AirPods.

"Music's the answer," she told me. "I've got a song that no matter how bad I'm feeling, it always does the job."

"Nice," I said. Nothing offensive in that.

She offered me a single AirPod. "Want to hear it?" she asked.

I couldn't say no, could I? Do that and she'd definitely sit somewhere else.

"OK," I said.

"You might not know it," she said. "It's an old one, but don't let that put you off. The singer is the only person who seems to know what's going on in my head sometimes. My mum played it for me a few months ago."

"Great," I replied, then wanted to kick myself for being so dull.

I took the AirPod and put it in my ear, then watched as she hit play on her phone. The song kicked in. It *was* old. And I thought it would be the last song I ever wanted to hear.

It was "These Arms of Mine". And the singer? Otis Redding.

But the weird thing was ... it sounded good. Sweet. Like I was hearing it for the very first time.

And you know what?

It helped.

"Oh, I know this," I said, smiling. "Otis Redding."

And then the most brilliant thing happened. At exactly the same time, we both said the same thing:

"The King of Soul."

I smiled. So did she, and I swear on my life she sat a little bit closer to me, like there was a cord joining our AirPods together.

We both listened, and as I looked out the bus window I saw a man with a perfect afro, moustache and black suit complete with ketchup stain, sitting on the wall of a pub called The Dock of the Bay, eating a kebab.

He looked at me, smiled and gave me a thumbs up.

My mouth fell open, and I turned to the girl.

"See that?" I said. "That guy over there?"

We both looked again. There was no one there.

But I didn't feel daft. And the girl didn't look bothered either. She just sort of ... smiled at me.

And the song played on.

Our books are tested
for children and young people by
children and young people.

Thanks to everyone who consulted on
a manuscript for their time and effort in
helping us to make our books better
for our readers.